P9-DHS-049

Tomie dePaola
Mice Squeak, We Speak

A Poem by Arnold L.Shapiro

G. P. Putnam's Sons · New York

Cats purr.

Lions roar.

Owls hoot.

Bears snore.

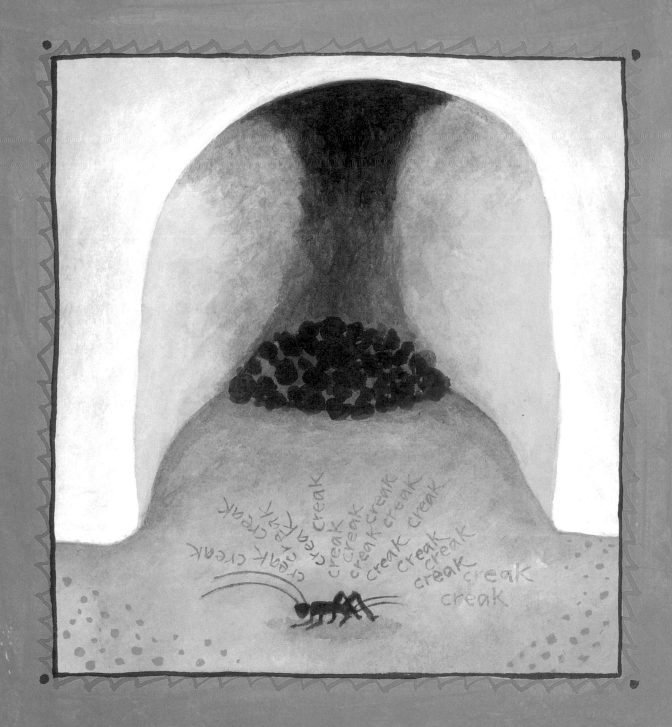

Crickets creak.

Mice squeak.

Sheep baa.

Monkeys chatter.

Cows moo.

Ducks quack.

COO-COO-COO-COO

Doves coo.

Pigs squeal.

Horses neigh.

Chickens cluck.

Flies hum.

Dogs growl.

Bats screech.

Coyotes howl.

Frogs croak.

Parrots squawk.

Bees buzz.

For Fraser Anthony
my Aussie godson
and his Mama and Papa, Jenny and Tony

Illustrations copyright © 1997 by Tomie dePaola

Text copyright © 1965 by Field Enterprises Educational Corporation.

Reprinted by permission of World Book, Inc. Original title "I Speak, I Say, I Talk."

All rights reserved. This book, or parts thereof, may not be reproduced in any form

without permission in writing from the publisher. G. P. Putnam's Sons, a division of

The Putnam & Grosset Group, 200 Madison Avenue, New York, NY 10016.

G. P. Putnam's Sons, Reg. U.S. Pat. & Tm. Off. Published simultaneously in Canada

Printed in Hong Kong by South China Printing Co. (1988) Ltd.

Designed by Patrick Collins and Donna Mark. Lettering by David Gatti

Library of Congress Cataloging-in-Publication Data

Shapiro, Arnold, 1934- Mice squeak, We speak/

by Arnold L. Shapiro; illustrated by Tomie dePaola. p. cm.

Summary: Illustrations and simple text describe the ways various animals

communicate, such as "Owls hoot," "Pigs squeal," and "Bees buzz."

[1. Animal sounds—Fiction.] I. dePaola, Tomie, ill. II. Title.

PZ7.S5294Mi 1997 [E]—dc21 96-54895 CIP AC

ISBN 0-399-23202-8

5 7 9 10 8 6 4